MW01228480

# THE ORC TRAPPER'S BRIDE

ORC OUTCASTS
BOOK 1

K.L. WYATT

This is a work of fiction. Names, characters, places, and incidents either are the product of the author's imagination or are used fictitiously. Any resemblance to actual persons, living or dead, events, or locales is entirely coincidental.

Copyright © 2023 by K.L. Wyatt

All rights reserved. No part of this book may be reproduced or used in any manner without written permission of the copyright owner except for the use of quotations in a book review. For more information, address: k.l.wyattauthor@gmail.com

eBook ISBN: 979-8-9872398-5-8
Paperback ISBN: 979-8-9872398-6-5

authorklwyatt.com

# CONTENT WARNING PAGE

For content warnings please scan here:

# DEDICATION

To the virgins with filthy minds

# 1

## RIVA

I've lived by two rules my entire life, to do as I am told and to not go into the swamp—today I've broken both.

"Riva!" My bridegroom's voice ricochets off of the mossy trees, filling my ears with his anger and hatred. I can't marry him, I *won't* marry him. Hamish is a despicable man who uses his power as our town's butcher against those he finds weak or less than. My parents told me to be happy with our arrangement, that I should be grateful even. In what world would I be happy marrying a man that takes pleasure from other people's pain?

I stupidly make the mistake of looking behind my shoulder and it causes me to trip over tangled roots which are sticking out of the ground. "Ah!" A small noise escapes me as I clatter to the ground in my overly puffy wedding gown. I curse under my breath; this ridiculous dress will not be the reason I am dragged back to town. I wince at the sight of my palms. There is dirt and twigs embedded in the cuts that I sustained from my fall but I have no time to stop. I shove down the burning sensation and instead use it to fuel me as I continue my sprint deeper into the swamplands. After all, whatever punishment Hamish thinks of for me will be a hundred times worse. As the light begins to fade and the mangled groves grow thicker, I still hear Hamish hot on my trail. I was a fool to think he wouldn't follow me here. His pride would never allow for a runaway bride. Hamish is used to getting what he wants, anyone who dares refuse him is dealt with in kind. I begin to hear multiple muffled voices shouting in the distance, Hamish isn't alone. I should have figured his loyal companions would have accompanied him on this hunt, because that is exactly what this is, a hunt, and I am the prey.

*Squish.* I suddenly feel my slippers fill with water and I am horrified when I look down—the ground is beginning to break away into various pools of water. I am frozen in fear as every story about the swamp comes rushing back into my mind. Alligators that drag you under the water, snakes whose bite will paralyze you, thousands of insects that carry diseases, yet the scariest of them all...orcs. The apex predator in this place—large green beasts that feast on their prey's bones.

I push down the tears that well in my eyes, threatening to escape. It isn't until this very moment that I realize how fucked I truly am. Either Hamish will kill me or something in this swamp will. Still, it is better to die trying to escape than at the hands of my bridegroom, or worse, spending my life with him.

Despite my better judgment, I take the necessary steps forward, making my decision to wade deeper into the swamp. My breathing becomes labored as the air is thick with humidity. In the short period of time I am already drenched with sweat. However, that is not the reason I begin to slow down, every step I take is more challenging than the last. The ground that isn't filled with water is a combination of moss, mud, and decaying matter. I will never make it. Taking another stride forward solidifies that. I try yanking my back foot up but nothing gives. In a panic I overcompensate, my weight causing me to go flying straight into the mud as I hear the popping release of my foot. "Please...*please*" I don't know who I'm crying out for but I can't stop the thick tears from rolling down my cheeks. I am cold, alone, scared, and absolutely filthy. This time I don't know if I can get up. I will never be able to outrun them. All of a sudden, I hear something peculiar, not Hamish or his men, but the sound of incessant knocking. Looking up, I see the cause of the racket. A black bird with a feathery red head pecking at one of the many mangled trees. Almost as if it knew it had been caught, the little bird flies away into the deep moss. Wait...the moss. I don't need to outrun my pursuers, I just need to hide from them! The revelation reinvigorates me, and despite my wretched appearance I give a wide smile to myself. It would seem like my prayers were answered. Thank you, little bird. Prying myself out of the mud and rot, I begin to map my pathway into the trees. I'll need to cross the dangerous water but luckily I see stones, logs, and exposed tangled roots from the trees in which I intend to seek refuge. I can still hear the men behind me despite my heart beating in my ears. I lost valuable time in the mud. I hastily attempt to cross the swamp waters, not allowing myself time to think about what lies just beneath its glassy surface. Instead, I focus on my next step, rock, log, another log, and a rock once more. The rocks are more sturdy but slimy. I lose my footing a few times and I ask myself if this obnoxiously large gown will serve as a life preserver. Maybe it will have its use after all.

Before I know it, I reach the final rock just before a small embankment. I've done it, I've made it across the dangerous water alive. It is a small win in comparison to everything that still has to happen to make my escape successful, but I would be lying if I said I wasn't overjoyed by my accomplishment. Jumping off the last rock, I land on the small, almost sandy embankment.

In my near delirium I begin speaking to myself, "Okay, Riva, now you just have to figure out how to climb these tre—"

Suddenly, something tightens around my ankle, dragging me up into the air. The world turns upside down, and to think I thought the swamp couldn't be any scarier. I let out a bloodcurdling scream as I try to work out what has a hold of me. I beg that whatever eats me does it quickly. The tears I thought were completely dried out come back at a rate I swear could create its own pool of water in this swamp. Despite my eyes going blurry from both my tears and the blood that is rushing to my head, I can feel that I am in some type of contraption and it isn't some animal that has grabbed me. However, what animals would be setting a trap out here? The realization makes my stomach hollow out and I begin to scream even louder. I don't care that Hamish and his men can hear me, I need out of this thing *now*!

That's when I hear it, the creature from my nightmare. It is only a few moments from hearing the first twigs snap that a giant green orc stands in front of me. I don't even try fighting as the world begins to go dark.

# 2

## KAL

I magine my surprise from hearing my trap bells ring, to seeing a human caught dangling by her foot. She shouldn't be here. Just then, my sharp pointed ears pick up on running in the distance. She isn't alone. Fascinating.

Her screams were piercing but now she hangs silent. Did she die? I caress her cheek to feel that she is still warm and her pulse beats rapidly against my palm— just unconscious then. She is so fair and delicate, my hands span the entire length of her head and it dawns on me just how vulnerable she is. It is amazing that the swamp hasn't already killed her. A low primal grunt escapes past my tusks. I will protect her.

She wears a puffy white dress that completely devours her petite frame. Dangling upside down causes the underskirts to fall, exposing her thin legs. My cock begins growing hard and my eyes can't help but to travel downwards, hoping to see a glimpse of something more than just her calves. I experience unwarranted frustration at the sight of her undergarments. If only she bared her pussy to me, then I would have an obligation to satisfy her.

Cupping my strained cock, I adjust myself to relieve some of the discomfort. Scoffing at her garments, I realize I have seen them before in my brief experiences observing humans. The women wear this dress when they are to become a wife.

My dick strains against my trousers once more, causing the discomfort to double. "My bride," I groan. All these years living in solitude have finally come to an end. I have captured my wife to be the ticket to my return to my clan. I've lived as an outcast since I came of age, with only my traps for entertainment and my hand for pleasure. Now, I have a womb to breed and a pussy to play with.

"Riva! Stop this foolish attempt to escape. Come out now, and I promise your punishment won't be nearly as bad," a human man screeches in the distance. Riva, that must be my bride's name. And punishment? A growl travels through my chest, traveling through my entire body. No one lays a hand on what is mine. I weigh my options. Do I show these fools exactly why humans do not step foot in this swamp? Or do I take my newly found treasure back to my tree cabin? I hone my hearing once more, and I pick up on multiple sets of footsteps. There are a few different men than just the one shouting. Gah! I spit. This isn't a problem for Kal the Trapper, but I risk one of them taking, or worse harming, my female. The decision is clear, I will take back my Riva to my cabin and make her my bride. Only once she is safe will I deal with these undeserving creatures.

I carry many weapons along my waist, but it is my knife that I currently hold in my hand. The blade slices through the rope with efficiency. It was just sharpened this morning. I grin to myself from just the thought of my weapons cutting through the human men that try and steal my bride.

Riva slumps in my arms as I untangle the tied piece of rope still attached to her ankle. Her pale face has become bright red and I am fascinated with how her skin changes color. I must remember to ask her about it. Not before long, she rests cradled in my arms as I carry her back to the cabin I've called home for these past long years. Her name plays over and over in my head. "Riva," I whisper to myself, trying to perfect it. She was my gift from the gods, my future wife, mother of my offspring, and ticket back into my beloved clan.

The swamp is perilous to those unfamiliar with its landscape, but luckily for my little Riva, I know this acreage like the back of my hand. I travel over logs, rock, and soaking moss with ease despite my large stature. I know every branch, plant, and lily pad within a radius of my cabin that I can essentially make the journey back with little to no effort. Instead I spend the energy observing my new bride some more. She seems to have a lot of hair, which is braided tightly into an updo. It is light but has darker tones throughout, which seem to be more or less prominent with the sun. My mind can't help but wonder at what she will look like with her hair free and wild—cascading down her back all the way to her bottom like a glorious waterfall.

My cock twitches at my own imagination and I selfishly lower her bottom so that my hardened length bumps into it as I walk. *Fuck*...I can feel the pre-cum begin soaking my britches. Trying to distract myself from my naughty thoughts, I focus on her eyebrows. They are a tad darker than her hair and a little bit thick. They hover over her mossy eyes which I only briefly got a glimpse of before she passed out. That was all the time I needed to know how dangerous they are. One look with those eyes and my wife-to-be will get anything she desires.

Before I know it, we arrive at the steps of my now

temporary home. Riva squirms slightly in my arms and I make sure to hold her tight as I ascend the mangled tree. Only once we reach the inside of my humble abode do I reluctantly pour her out of my arms and into my straw bed. Taking a few steps back, I am able to take in the sight of her body from a distance. She is absolutely filthy and utterly all mine.

The pressure in my trousers has reached its unbearable limit. My cock demands to be released from these confines. And with Riva now safe, who am I to deny myself after all these years? Grabbing a nearby chair, I sit in front of my female and imagine it is her slim little fingers that begin to untie my garments. I am only able to loosen a few before my cock springs forward, demanding to be taken care of. I compare my hardened length to her small frame and question if I will be able to fit. Fuck, even two of my thick fingers could fill her up. Almost on cue, beads of pre-cum gush from the head of my dick, reminding me that my body will find a way to fit. Her tight little holes might need some training, but she will learn to accommodate my thickness and length.

Suddenly, my little Riva starts to stir and I can't help my own debauchery. I pump my cock up and down as her breathing changes and her eyes begin to flutter open. Little do I expect the deafening scream my bride lets out at the sight of her new bridegroom.

# 3

## RIVA

Nightmare, I am in a nightmare. It is the only explanation for why I am in a strange cabin with an orc brute mere steps away. Quickly, my screams are silenced with this hand, the hand he was just using to pleasure himself. I can't help but to take a deep inhale of his musk, and to my own horror it is intoxicating.

"Shh...be calm." His guttural voice is surprisingly soothing. "With me you shall only scream from pleasure and not fear."

Another spike of terror registers through my body but he responds by holding me tighter, an unexpectedly effective method to console me.

"I am going to let go of you now. No more screaming, okay?" he explains calmly while I fixate on his features. I should be repulsed. Here stands a real life orc, the creatures from my scary stories. Instead, I'm transfixed by his primal beauty—his silk black hair with shaved sides, a full beard with sharp protruding tusks, and those lips...for my mind wanders and I imagine what they would taste like.

A deep chuckle fills the room. "Do you like what you see, Riva?"

Just as quickly as it came, the allure is broken. "How do you know my name?"

"You seem to have many admirers wandering the forest. Unfortunately for them, I found you first." His voice remains steady but I feel his eyes devouring me.

Hamish and his men, he must have heard them calling for me. That still doesn't explain how I got here or what happened after I was ensnared in this orc's trap.

"Are they..." I hold my breath, waiting for his response

"No, but they will be. Anyone who tries to hurt my bride will suffer the consequences." He speaks so matter-of-factly that I almost don't question his absurd declaration.

"Bride!?" I exclaim

Gone is his restful posture. Now a predator stalks in front of me, "Yes, Riva, you are to be my bride. Too long have I been away from my people, outcast to live alone in the swamp until I find a female to wed and breed." He whispers the last part directly into my ear, sending shivers down my spine. "For years I have begged the gods to give me a woman, and today those prayers were answered."

"D-don't you want...an orc female?" I stutter out my question from both fear and infatuation. Maybe too much blood rushed to my head.

"There are very few orc females left." He tilts my head to the side with his large palm and gives my neck a small lap of his tongue, causing me to moan. "My bride is so sensitive. Tell me, are you this sensitive everywhere?" He begins moving his hand lower, and before I lose all my senses completely I jump out of his bed. Unfortunately for me, I stand too quickly that I feel like I might faint. Before I clatter to the ground, a strong presence holds me in place. "I've got you, wife."

Now, I don't know if it is because Hamish was so cruel or that I was the forgotten child or that I nearly just died in the swamp but those four words make me want to melt into a puddle. As if he could see my desperation in my eyes, the orc in front of me decides to sit down back in his chair, but to my surprise brings me with him. To my disappointment, at some point he seemed to have slipped his cock back into trousers. It is probably for the better, I am clearly not thinking straight.

His thick fingers caress my chin and direct me to look at him. "I apologize for my brutish behavior, it has been a *very* long time since I have had the company of a female." He studies my eyes and I can't help but be enamored by his gold-like eyes. "But I promise you, Riva, as my wife you will be clothed, fed, safe, and loved. The only thing I ask in return is that you carry my offspring, that you allow me to fill you with my seed until you bear me a kit."

His words should be like water on a flame but instead it sends fire to my loins. This orc wants to give me a life I have always desired...but it is crazy. I couldn't possibly marry and start a family with an orc.

"I-I can't. I was trying to run away from my bridegroom, not find another."

His angry growl vibrates throughout my entire body. "You are scared of him. Scared enough to run into the swamplands where you were sure to die. And for that, it will be his blood, not yours. He is not worthy of you but I am." He rubs my thigh as he firmly declares revenge for my honor. I am struck with silent awe...for the first time in my life I feel safe. Who would have thought that I would feel the most seen in the swamplands with an orc? Maybe I did die earlier and this is just a figment of my imagination.

"My name is Kal, by the way." He doesn't stop his gentle massage of my thigh and I can't help my eyes flutter. "Say it...say my name, Riva."

"Kal," I whisper, and I feel his hardened length twitch beneath me.

"By the gods, you say my name like a prayer," he groans

Both my exhaustion and delusion become greater under his erotic touch and I begin to lean my head against his chest.

"My little human, look at you, how can you deny being my bride?" His fingers begin to migrate in between my thighs. "Oh I know, you need me to prove myself. Prove that I can bring you great pleasure." I don't stop him as his fingers graze over my covered privates. I should be embarrassed that the fabric is soaked with my juices, but I am far too tired to care. His fingers move back up to the entrance of my undergarments only to quickly descend again, only this time under them.

"Prove that this pretty little pussy is *mine*." He cups me with his massive paw and I release the breath I didn't realize I was holding. Another growl rumbles through me but this time it is anger, it is...discomfort. He doesn't let go of my pussy and I shift positions and lock eyes with him. He doesn't need to use his words, I can feel his cock fighting the restraints of his trousers. Without thinking, I reach down and release his throbbing member—for a brief moment I am again shocked by his sheer girth and length while Kal lets out a groan.

"Look at your little hand around my monster cock," he teases, but before I can respond in kind he begins to circle my clit with his thick forefinger.

"Ahhhh!" A shot of ecstasy fills my veins from his touch

"That is the only kind of scream I want to hear in this cabin." He nuzzles his tusks into the crook of my neck and continues his maddening touch. I feel frozen in ecstasy but for some reason I want to prove my control over him. Before I know it I attempt to wrap my fingers around his width, causing a pool of pre-cum to leak out.

"Fuck!" Kal roars. "So the little human wants to play with my big cock. Agree to marry me and it is all yours." He suddenly slips his finger between my folds and into my cunt, already completely filling me.

"Oh gods!" I cry as his single finger stretches me,

"It's simple, Riva..." He begins to buck slightly into my hand. "Become my bride and let me fill you with my seed and we will return to my clan where I will take care of you for the rest of our days." His words only increase my pleasure and already I am in the danger zone of coming.

"Say yes, my human, and I will make you feel like this every day." He promptly uses his thumb to encircle my clit while his fingers move rhythmically in and out of me, causing the pressure to build to my breaking point.

"YESSS!" I scream while a wave of pure bliss washes over me.

"Yes to what, Riva? Say it? Fucking say it!" he demands as he relentlessly paws at my soaking wet cunt.

"Yes, I will marry you! Yes, I will give you offspring! Yes, I want you to breed me," I scream, and I feel like I am releasing demons. "Yes, I want you to stretch me with your fat orc cock! Yes, I want you to fill me to the brim with your seed!" I don't know what has come over me but I keep screaming everything I shouldn't desire but I do. Next thing I know, Kal is letting out a scream of his own and a white stringy substance erupts from his cock, covering me. He bucks wildly into my hand but grabs the back of my neck to bring me into an all-consuming kiss. It is a kiss like I've never experienced before—raw, primal, demanding, but also loving. I return his passion in kind as I push my lips into his tusks. His hot sticky cum continues to pelt me, covering my dress in a new layer of white.

We both attempt to catch our breath when someone

screams, "Riva, you nasty fucking whore!" No, not some-one. Hamish. He found me. I am overcome with pure panic and jump from Kal's lap.

Kal bares his tusks in anger and stands from the chair, except he is confident and sure of himself—this is the monster I was warned about. But unlike those monsters, he pulls me into his chest and kisses my head. "Don't worry, little wife."

Almost on cue, I hear Hamish and his men scream, bells within the cabin ring, and then...silence. I can't help the tears that form in my eyes. "Are they—"

"They will never harm you again," he says simply, but as the tears start to roll down my reddened cheeks, he explains, "You see, I am a trapper. I have the ability to capture live prey, dead prey, or to kill prey with my contraptions. Those weak men never stood a chance and neither did you."

His words should frighten me, but instead they ignite a fire within my soul.

# 4

## KAL

The human men never stood a chance. My home is protected with various different traps, some deadly and some not—either way their fate was sealed the second they tried to harm my sweet little bride. Riva clutches my chest with her tiny little paws and shields her face from the deceased as we walk by them. She still fears these men even after their death. Anger heats my blood and in the moment I wish to resurrect them only to slaughter them again. Their bodies lie pierced by many wooden stakes protruding from a hole. Their faces are twisted with fear and agony, which gives me slight reprieve in my anger. I will deal with their bodies later—right now I have a female to claim.

"Open your eyes, little one." I tuck a loose strand of

her sandy light hair behind her ear as I cradle her in my arms like I did when I first found her—I could most definitely get used to this. Her eyes flutter while they take time to adjust. Luckily in the swamp there isn't intense lighting.

"What will you do with them?" she whispers

I take time to answer her response earnestly. I will not lie to my bride. "I will feed them to the alligators." She squirms in response so I grab her chin. "You cannot bury the dead in the swamp. Instead we give it back to its inhabitants." Her eyes study mine, and for the first time I feel uneasy. I want to know what she is thinking and more importantly what she thinks about *me.*

"I can walk, you know."

"It is dangerous, my bride. The swamplands are filled with murderous creatures, including me. My traps are set all across this territory." I don't like the distance she is putting between us. I want back the fiery Riva that just came all over my fingers. "Besides, I like carrying you."

Suddenly, her cheeks grow red and she turns her face away from me. Before I can ask her about her new-found shyness, she asks me about our wedding ceremony.

"Where are we going? I-I mean I know we are to be wed but how do we do that in a land like this?" She looks around pensively at the place I've always called my home. "Are we going to have an orc officiator?"

"A what?" My bride asks many questions and I don't understand some of her words

"A wedding officiator, you know, someone who says the words of a ceremony, making a union legally binding."

I chuckle at such a ridiculous notion. "Is this what humans do? You are such strange creatures."

"Hey—"

"Orcs are not bound with words, we are bound by our souls." I cut her off in order to provide a clearer explanation of the ceremony we are to participate in. "In the heart of the swamp lies The Chosen, an ancient tree that grows on the smallest island. That is where we head now. Upon our arrival we will feast on its fruits and I will claim each and every one of your holes." She lets out a gasp and I can't help my cock's barbaric response to her fear. "Once you are filled with my seed, hopefully The Chosen will bless our union with a pregnancy."

"I...what if I cannot..." Her words trail off but I understand her question well enough

"You will, my bride. I can smell that you are fertile." I growl and lower her ass against my strained cock. "After all, orc seed is very strong, that is why we have strong sons."

"What if we have a girl?" she asks, so earnestly it is a miracle I don't shove her to the ground and fuck her tight cunt.

"It is very unlikely, my sweet bride." I don't hide my sorrow in my response.

"Why not?"

"I told you earlier, there are not many orc females left. The elders do not know why, but around a hundred years ago there was a great increase in male orcs born. With the lack of females, our population is rapidly declining."

"That is why they won't let you live in the clan without a wife..." she deduces. "They are forcing you out of your home so you can find a female to start a family."

I nod. "It may seem like a harsh punishment, but it is a necessary one. My dear Riva, if we do not find females to breed then my people may cease to exist."

She studies my eyes and I have the overwhelming desire to kiss her supple lips. Knowing I can't trust myself, I force myself to look ahead on our journey. Luckily for me, we have finally reached our destination. Pushing away the moss that shields the pathway, I reluctantly place Riva on her feet.

"By the gods..." she whispers in wonder, "this place is unlike anything I have ever seen before." And she is right—The Chosen One is unlike any tree in existence.

Purple veins thread throughout its trunk into the branches that are filled with willowy vines that produce delectable, round, purple fruit. Its roots are firmly anchored on a miniature island surrounded by plush grass.

"It is beautiful, is it not?"

'It is more than beautiful." She pauses to find the correct word. "It is…magical."

I study her excitement and adoration. The Chosen One may be magical, but Riva is the true enchantress. I lead her down the pathway, onto the grass, and up to one of the thousands of fruit-bearing vines.

I steady her petite body in front of my own while I reach around her to pluck one of the juicy purple fruits. Riva only stands as high as my lower pecs and when she leans her weight into me, I feel my hard length span up to her mid back. To my surprise she shifts her weight again…and then again…

A moan escapes my tusks. My sweet bride is teasing me. I tear the fresh fruit in half and bring it to her soft pliable lips. "Eat, my bride. The fruit's effects will determine if we are suited mates. Either we will be consumed by lust or driven by hatred." She is only reluctant for a second before taking her first bite. I experience fear for a brief second before shoving my doubts deep down. The human female has already driven me mad with yearning, this claiming will be successful—it has to be.

"Mmmm." She closes her eyes as she moans and I am transfixed by her expressions.

I lean down to her ear and whisper, "I imagine your pussy is even juicier."

She clenches her legs together at my words while I finish my half of the fruit—her sweet cunt will definitely be juicier.

She takes another bite as I use my legs to part hers. She lets out a small gasp but continues eating The Chosen One's fruit. I have heard stories of The Claiming before I was outcast, that the fruit causes a lustful frenzy that can only be satiated after breeding each of the spouse's holes.

Riva's body starts to heat and I feel a wave of ecstasy wash over me. "Are you going to let me make this mouth mine?" I wrap my hand around her fragile neck and use my thumb to caress her lips.

"Y-yes," she whispers

"What was that? I can't hear you."

"Yes, my mouth is yours," she states a little more firmly.

"Not quite yet, little bride, but soon it will be." I shove my leg into the shallow sensitive bit behind her knee, which causes her to fall to the ground. I feel a squeak vibrate throughout her throat as I still clasp it in my hand. She is totally vulnerable and completely at my mercy as she sits on her knees in front of me. The thought makes the constriction of my trousers against my cock unbearable. I need to free myself. Shoving my bride forward, she lands on her hands with a grunt while I release my hardened length from its confines.

"Fuck, Riva, do you feel how hard you make me?" I rub my slick pre-cum cock against her clothing-covered ass.

"Mhm, you are so big." Her voice slides against my skin, making me feel both hot and cold. She is driving me fucking crazy. She snuggles her ass into my length and I can't control the growl that fills my chest.

"What are you waiting for?" Riva begins to reach under her gown to remove her undergarments. Her words are laced with lust, which tells me that The Chosen has blessed this union. I should be rubbing my shaft against her bare ass but I fear that her exposed pussy would cause me to prematurely combust.

"Patience, my bride. First, I will claim that pretty little mouth of yours. Only then can I move on to breeding that sweet pussy." I palm her cunt in my hand to make sure she understands who it belongs to. "And finally, I will stretch your tight little asshole until you can fit every inch of me."

Riva clenches her legs together at my words, moaning, "Yes...yes, take me."

She doesn't need to say more, as I make my way over to face her. Even on my knees she has to sit up partially in order to reach my cock. Beads of pre-cum roll down my shaft and she licks her lips in response. Once more, her fingers attempt to clasp around my cock but only cover about half of the diameter.

"Kal..." She says my name laced with concern and looks up at me with her big mossy eyes. "I really don't know if I can fit this in my mou—"

Those eyes are my fucking undoing. I can no longer hold myself back and use my dick to silence her doubts. My girth silences her initial protests and it takes every ounce of my willpower to keep still.

"You will take this cock, Riva, do you understand me?" I've observed that Riva relaxes when I am in control. Uncertainty allows for both fear and trepidation to plague her mind. It is no surprise to me that her body begins to relax in response to my command. Only when she nods her agreement do I remove my length from her petite mouth.

Taking a deep gasp of air, she exclaims, "I will take as much of your cock as I can."

"No." I shove my length back into her mouth, pushing past her previous limit. "You will take every inch of it." Again, her body relaxes further, allowing me to slip down even further.

"*Fuck*, Riva. Yes, just like that," I groan, tilting my head back. Her mouth feels better than anything I could possibly imagine—I fear her pussy might transcend me.

Pulling out once more, I allow her to catch her breath. Wrapping my hand back around her throat, I can feel her heart racing.

"Let me try again...*please*." Now she is begging me? Oh, this is just too much. Chuckling, I give my sweet bride what she desires and slide my rod back down her throat. She spreads her knees slightly and uses her left hand to grasp my thick thigh in order to remain sturdy.

"Oh, so my bride wants it a little rougher." She moans and nods her reply. "You only get more when you use that spare hand to pleasure yourself."

My mouth begins to water as I watch Riva's hand disappear under her undergarments. Only when I feel the soft vibration of her moans do I begin sliding ever so slightly in and out of her mouth. After a few strokes she starts to get a feel for my member in her mouth and begins using her tongue in my creative ways. She is practically milking the pre-cum out of me as the base of my shaft begins to collect more and more of the creamy substance.

"*Ooooh*, Riva!" I cry out and my thrusts become

rougher. "See, all you needed was a bit of positive rein-forcement." My cock reaches the back of her throat, causing her to gag, but I don't stop. I give my bride exactly what she wants.

"That's it, take every inch of me. Take every inch of my orc cock."

Tears stream down her pink flushed cheeks as I relentlessly fuck her throat. On my next thrust her tiny little mouth reaches the base of my shaft. Instead of pulling back quickly for another thrust, I hold her head in place and watch as she starts making erratic movements.

"Is my sweet bride coming? " I tease, still holding her head in place. "Is my bride coming while she is choking on my cock?"

Full body spasms rock through her and although her screams are silenced by my thick rod, I feel their vibrations. Once I feel her body go limp, I let go of her head and she desperately gasps for air. My cock yearns for her warmth once more but I know I need to let my little human rest.

"Not your bride," she chokes out, staring defiantly at me.

"What did you say?" My tone grows dark in response to her statement.

"Not your bride," she declares again. "Your *wife*."

My eyes widen in shock and before I know it, my cock is filling her mouth again. Her declaration has crazed me. "That's right, Riva, you are my fucking wife." My bucking is becoming harder and more volatile but now she uses both hands on my thighs to steady herself. "You are all mine. This mouth is all *mine.*"

Her moans send me over the edge and I explode in her mouth. I imagine my roar can be heard throughout the swamplands as I continue to pump more hot liquid down her throat. I take in the sight of my wife as my seed leaks out of her nose and mouth and it is absolutely stunning.

Once she releases me, the remainder of the cum that she couldn't swallow pours from her mouth. She is so fucking beautiful, so...*perfect.* I am in complete awe of the female in front of me.

I am stunned into silence as she looks up at me with a meek smile and admiration in her eyes. It is at this very moment that I realize I would wait for the rest of my life in these swamps for her and *only* her. She isn't just any human female, she is *my* human female. The other half of my soul. My *mate.*

Although Riva may have fallen into one of my traps, it is she who has ensnared my heart.

# 5

## RIVA

I'm wet, horny, and covered from head to toe in Kal's seed. I stare into the eyes of my now husband. He has retreated back into his mind, a place I am not yet welcome. Before I can use the opportunity to overthink, he bends down and crushes his lips against mine. His tusks are flush against my cheeks and I've oddly enough grown fond of the sensation. I'm surprised at my husband's self-control. He is in no rush despite all those years alone. Instead, he takes his time exploring my mouth with his tongue. Each stroke is purposeful...mindful...and teasing. I never expected my own impatience in this situation. I—well, I'm not quite sure what I am expecting. Maybe that he would sling me to the ground and claim my pussy immediately. My core tightens at the mere thought of his savageness.

. . .

AS IF HE can read my thoughts, Kal rumbles into my mouth, "Are you not satisfied, my wife?" His wife. My heart soars at his declaration. I am drunk on my lust for him, and it feels like I am unable to get my fill.

"Not until you finish your claim, husband." My voice is raspy after his rough fucking but still holds firm. "Ah, well, I must see to it then." He tilts my neck to the side and licks from my collarbone to my ear, "I didn't realize you were just as eager to carry my kit."

His whisper creates goosebumps across my skin both because of the sensation of his hot breath and his words. The truth is, I do want to carry his kit. I've always wanted to be a mom, to bring a child into the world where they would be loved and seen, never forgotten.

In response, I surprise him by cupping his face beneath his black beard. My husband is not familiar with receiving gentle affection—that's okay, neither am I.

A low menacing growl leaves his throat and his eyes promise another rough encounter. Bring it on. I feel my clit throb in anticipation and I somehow grow wetter. Before I know it, Kal is grabbing my wedding gown, completely tearing it in half. My breasts are suddenly met with the heavy hot air and I gasp as my sensitive nipples harden.

"So fucking beautiful," he muses before suckling my breast in his mouth. "Soon these will be heavy with milk."

Gush, another wet gush rolls down my thighs. "Please, Kal." I need it with a desperation I didn't know was possible.

I let his menacing chuckle fill my body as he flips in the other direction until my ass sits right before his cock.

"This won't do," he exclaims, referring to my under-garments." This won't do at all. I hereby ban you from ever wearing these." In honor of his declaration, I hear a ripping sound and then feel the rush of fresh air across my exposed cunt.

"That is much better. You see..." He rubs his thick forefinger down my soaking wet slit and I can't contain my moan. "I want access to this pussy at all times."

He circles my clit a few times and I squirm under his touch until I feel something large press against my ass. I do my best to control my breathing but the anticipation is killing me. Kal slides his massive member right in front of my entrance and I fear once more that he won't fit.

"Relax your body, Riva, you are going to take me just like you did with your mouth"

Memories of our rough encounter flash through my mind, creating additional lubricant.

"You are so fucking wet for me." And with that I can feel him trying to enter. "Mmm and so tight too"

This isn't the first time I am having sex, but it is the first time I am taking something so large. Kal grabs my ass in order to use his brute force for his invasion.

"Ahhhhhh!" The thickness of his cock starts to stretch me open. "Kal!"

"Yes, that's it, take my orc cock"

I am filled with a multitude of sensations, tingles, pain, pressure, and ecstasy.

"Mhm, yes, I can feel you." I try to scream my encouragement. The feeling of him inching deeper inside of me is unfamiliar and yet euphoric—I need more!

Once the throbbing end of his member is through, the rest slides in with ease.

"Fuck! You are so godsdamn tight."

"Yes...yes! Don't stop"

"Never!"

The world becomes one big blur and Kal's thrusts become harder and more relentless. My core starts building to an orgasm but I can't do anything but lie there as he claims my pussy.

"Don't"—slap—"stop"—slap. His heavy balls start slapping my ass on every thrust and I am only a few strokes away from exploding into pieces.

"This sweet cunt is mine!" he exclaims, and I've never felt him more feral. "Now, what do you want?"

"I want you to fuck me!" I scream in pleasure. I am so close.

"No, what do you fucking want, Riva?"

"I want you to breed me! I want you to fill my pussy to the brim with your seed over and over again until I carry your kit in my belly."

My words make him lose control and he bellows into the sky as a hot spurt of cum blasts my cervix wall. The buildup of pressure is too great and I finally find release, "Kal, I'm coming!"

"That's it, my little wife, come for me! Come on your orc husband's cock"

His words break me into smaller pieces as another orgasm bursts throughout my body. I can feel my heartbeat in my head and everything starts to feel extremely heavy. Before I can flop to the ground, Kal wraps his arms around my waist, pulling me into his arms.

"Good girl," he coos, and his praise makes me feel squishy on the inside.

"This feels right, you and me like this." He waves down at our bodies. I couldn't agree more. Something about us defies logic. How can you meet someone in such strenuous circumstances and still find yourself utterly enamored?

I try to steady my breathing as Kal's fingers gravitate towards my pussy, where a stream of hot cum continues to trickle out.

"Mmm, that's a beautiful bred cunt," he growls and uses two of his fingers to push some of his seed back inside of me.

It isn't long before the tingly sensation between my thighs returns. Kal's cock has remained hard since....well, since I met him.

I can feel his rock-hard rod begin to twitch against my ass as he brings his fingers up to mouth. "Have a taste of our juices together."

He feeds me our mingled cum like it is a three-course meal. The juices melt on my tongue with a mixture of flavors that are salty, sweet, intoxicating—

"Ahhhhh!" A scream rips through me like his cock does to my ass. "Kal! It hurts!" Panic washes over me in waves and my asshole feels like it's on fire.

"Shhh, relax into me, Riva. Just breathe, I'm not moving until you adjust to me."

My breathing is erratic but I realize he isn't lying. He

is completely still, with the head of his throbbing cock poking through my sphincter. As I start to control my breathing, the ring of fire begins to subside.

"Look at how good you are at taking my cock in your ass," he growls in my ear, and my pussy clenches empty air.

"I promise to take it better each time, husband!" I cry from the pain that has oddly turned into pleasure. "You are huge!"

"Riva, if you keep speaking like that, I'm—"

"You are going to come? But you haven't finished training my tight ass to take your monster rod." My own words take me by surprise but I revel in my power over him. That I can drive him over the edge before he is ready.

"Fuckkkkk!" His pleasure rings in my ear for the third time this evening and yet just as much creamy seed fills my ass.

He pulls out only the small length he was able to fit inside of me, lowering me to the ground completely. I feel a shift in the air around me. Nothing explicit has changed and yet everything has. I think back to the juicy purple fruit, the longing desire, and the barbaric claiming—that was it, we are officially wedded to each other.

It is strange that the idea of something like marriage

was so terrifying to me simply because of the man, but now I don't have a man, I have an orc.

"It is complete. You are officially *mine* just as it was intended to be. We shall rest here for some time, my wife. Then we will clean you up and make our way back to my clan," he grumbles, trying to collect his breath.

A small word, *my*, seems so meaningless but in that moment it feels like a slap in the face. It shouldn't bother me and yet it does. Doubts begin pouring into my mind as I start replying to every interaction we have had. Of course I know he was using me to return to his clan but...fuck, he is using me. My throat constricts and my palm becomes sweaty. What the fuck was I even thinking? Kal senses my mood shift and with the force of his hand on my chin, directs me to look at him.

"What troubles you, wife?"

"Nothing, I am just tired," I lie.

He narrows his eyes suspiciously at me but when I give him my best fake smile, he doesn't push the subject. Instead, he pulls my upper body down to the ground with him so that we can sleep. It's amazing how I am able to feel his heartbeat slow and his breath steady just simply through touch. He has fallen asleep after being completely spent. I take pride in knowing I am a huge cause of it. I am, however, not as lucky. Life has changed rapidly and suddenly. In truth I don't know how to handle it.

Looking over my shoulder, I see my handsome orc husband sleeping peacefully. I take the opportunity to slip out of his embrace and stand for the first time in what feels like ages. Especially now that I have a husband that likes to carry me everywhere. My mind races with thoughts as I stare between The Chosen One tree and Kal. This has been the craziest day of my life, I just need to go for a walk and clear my head.

....

THE FARTHER I travel up the footpath away from the sacred tree and my husband, I realize how much faster it is traveling with Kal. His long legs allow for long strides versus my short legs that require me to take many more steps to reach the same distance. Pushing my way through the covered entrance and exit, I am confronted by the sheer difference of the swamp compared to our little oasis. Despite my better judgment, I decide to press on, telling myself that a little walk will be good for my head. So far, no luck. In fact I feel like the farther away I am from Kal, the more anxiety I feel. He promised to always keep me safe, and being alone in such a harsh environment is making me realize he was already keeping his promise.

I shake my head. He is keeping me safe because I am valuable to him, but not in the way I wish to be. It is foolish to think that his happiness is anything more than his ability to return home. What's worse is that I can't even blame him. Of course he wants to return to his people. I can't imagine being an outcast. My situation is different, I fled, but Kal? Kal was forced to leave everything and everyone behind unless he found a female. Insecurity starts to creep in. What if he doesn't even like humans? What if deep down he wishes I was an orc, like him? Again, I could hardly blame him. I rub my hands over my face and take in my appearance in the glassy water. I am hardly something to desire. I continue along the embankment, doing my best to shove away the negative thoughts. After all, I should be happy. Yesterday I was engaged to a hateful man but now, I have someone who saved me, who is kind to me. I just...well, I think I may have fallen for this orc beast.

Suddenly, a small deer appears, walking up to the pool of swamp water and drinking from it. I can't help but to smile as I watch a creature so similar to me exist in this harsh world. The distraction gives my mind a reprieve from its spiraled thoughts which I am grateful for.

*SPLASH*

The once still water now ripples and a giant reptilian creature jumps from its depths, catching the small deer in its fangs. I can't scream, can't move, can't do anything. It all happens so fast the poor thing didn't stand a chance. The alligator snaps its jaws, ensuring its prey is killed before dragging it into the depths.

Finally my body catches up with my brain and kicks into gear. I need to get back to Kal, *now,* before I'm next! Unfortunately, my state of shock turns into panic, causing me to lose my sense of direction. I can't just stand here...damn it, Riva, just go!

I start running but I can't escape the constant pools of water. Now knowing what lurks beneath them, I realize just how stupid it was to wander on my own. Tears form in my eyes and I begin to hyperventilate from the fear. Here I am once again running in a now ripped-to-shreds wedding gown through the swamps. Should I call for Kal? Will he even hear me? Or will I just draw the attention of another terrifying beast? Instead, I settle on controlling my sobs.

*SNAP*

This is it. Something has found me and now stalks me through the swamp. I am a goner. I try looking behind me as I sprint forward but for the second time today, something wraps around my ankle, dragging me upward. A trap. I am in one of Kal's traps, only this time whatever chases me will eat me before he can ever find—

"Riva!" Kal roars as he emerges from the mangled mossy trees and into my sight. It wasn't just any beast that stalked me, it was *my* beast, my husband. My relief just causes more sobs to wrack through my body. I have never been so happy to see someone in my entire life. Except, the feeling is not reciprocated. Kal is angry...very angry.

"What the fuck do you think you are doing, wife?" he seethes. "You think you can run from me? Escape me? Worse, you try to do it after our claiming ceremony!" I can see the genuine hurt in his eyes.

'N-no—" I try to spit out but I can't control my breathing

"No? Then what are you doing out here? It is one thing to run but now you are lying!' His accusations feel like a punch to the gut as I continue to dangle from his rope. Clearly, Kal has no interest in taking me down, at least not yet.

"I-I'm not lying!" I shout, and more tears fall to the moist ground. "I just needed to think!"

"Think about what? How to kill yourself?"

"About us! About...how you feel about me." I hiccup. This is so embarrassing.

He stalks forward and with a low growl he asks, "What about us?"

"You only wanted to marry me so you could go home." I close my eyes so I don't have to see his disappointment. "I understand and I shouldn't be so selfish but I...I want it to mean more. I want us to mean more. I guess I had just hoped you would feel the same way I feel about you."

Kal blows out a deep breath and asks, "You think I don't care about you?"

Peeking open my eyes, I am surprised by the expression I find. Hurt. That hurt quickly turns back to anger. "You are my wife! And now after the claiming, you are my heart! Yes, we can now return to my clan, but our marriage has changed everything. I don't need my people...I need you. I want you. I choose you!" His words melt my heart and my tears of fear quickly turn into tears of happiness. Kal leans closer and his hot breath brushes over my exposed pussy. It is completely depraved but his words send a deep shiver of desire to my core.

"We can live in my cabin for the rest of our days,

whatever will prove my feelings to you. But you can never try to escape me. Do you understand? I cannot lose you, my wife," he growls. "For if you go, I go. Your heart is now my heart. I cannot stand to be without you."

"Kal..." I whisper

"Promise me. Promise you will never try to leave me again!" He hovers directly above my pussy now, teasing me.

"I promise!" I cry

His tongue wastes no time lapping at my juices and I let out another cry, but this time from pleasure. He is relentless, like my cunt is his very first meal in days. He makes sure to focus on my clit, which causes my core to constrict and my pussy to clench. He quickly fills the empty void in between my legs with his fingers.

"I told you this sweet pussy is mine!"

"Yes...*yes*, Kal, my pussy is all yours!"

I attempt to sit up but to no avail. Gravity works against me. But suddenly a very large opportunity presents itself. Kal's protruding member pleads to be released from his trousers. I paw his ties and he lets out a deep moan into my soaking wet cunt. I struggle with the strings as I hang upside down but eventually free his cock. I waste no time shoving my favorite toy back into my mouth. I need to make it up to my husband.

"*Fuck*, wife!" Kal moans and it only encourages me to take more of him.

It doesn't take long for both of us to reach our climaxes. My pussy clenches tightly around his meaty fingers that relentlessly fuck me.

"That's it, wife, come for me."

My screams are muffled by his cock as a large orgasm consumes my body. Kal begins to buck in and out of my mouth, which is quickly met with a geyser of cum. He rubs his juice-covered fingers across my face. "Such a dirty little wife."

I can't help but to chuckle. My mind is finally at peace. Kal cuts me down from his trap and I land in his arms.

"That is the second time I have been in one of your traps."

"And it won't be the last," he teases, wiping my semen-covered face. The gesture is oddly symbolic for our relationship.

"Kal..." I hesitate. "I think I love you."

He only looks me earnestly in my eyes and responds, "Well, I *know* I love you."

# EPILOGUE: KAL

It didn't take long before Riva fell pregnant. After all, I was diligent about her breeding. I make my way back to our home, which rests at the center of our clan. My people received Riva with open arms. In fact they tend to be a tad overbearing. Our clan elders dote on her and claim she is the beginning to a new age of prosperity.

I smile down at the animals I was able to trap today. Not only do I need to provide for my pregnant wife but also contribute to the clan. Luckily for both, I am an excellent trapper and clearly not a humble one.

*Whoosh...whoosh*

I hear rumbling from the bushes and I'm immediately set on edge, pulling out my axe to prepare to slaughter anything that attempts to harm me.

"At ease, brother." The familiar voice is quickly met with the familiar face.

"Evrin." I relax my shoulders as I come face to face with the male I once called my friend. "What are you doing here? You know you shouldn't be this close to the clan village." My reprimand falls flat. Before Riva, I too watched our clan from a distance, always to remain hidden.

'Your female—"

A warning growl fills the air. "Do not dare speak of my wife!"

"Where did you find her?" He wears his desperation like a mask and a sudden wave of pity washes over me. Evrin is an outcast, and like all outcasts we were never to interact with each other for fear of fighting over a female. The orc population already has declining numbers, it would be stupid to contribute to the crisis.

"My human became ensnared in one of my traps," I answer honestly. His disappointment is evident, Evrin is a blacksmith, not a trapper. Even if he was, it was unlikely he would ever catch a human—my Riva was sent to me by the gods. My mind wanders to her as I look at Evrin and I realize just how lucky I am.

"You will find a female, Evrin. I swear it." I try to reassure him.

"Thank you, Kal. As you can imagine, the news of

your claim has spread like wildfire with the outcasts." The news doesn't surprise me. To be an outcast is to spend every waking moment thinking about a mate. If there is news of a claimed female, every outcast will be made aware. There is a brief silence before he asks, "Does she carry your kit?"

"Yes," I state honestly, knowing my words are a stab to the gut.

He only nods his acknowledgement before walking towards what I can only assume is his own lonely cabin in the swamp.

I watch as he disappears in the distance and then continue on my route back to my home. I only make it a few steps into town before I hear shouting and screaming coming from our tree cabin. Panic rushes throughout my body—Riva!

"Girls!" a town elder exclaims as I bust down the door and grab my wife. I am met with tears and...smiles?

"What is going on?" I grunt

"Girls!" the town elder, Izel, screams again.

"What girls?" My brain is not processing the events fast enough

"Oh Kal, you daft fool, you are having girls!" Izel brushes me aside and dotes on Riva instead. Girls...girls! I am too stunned to speak and my wife giggles at my response. "Are you okay, husband?"

"I am more than okay!" I exclaim. "We are having girls—"

The realization hits me like a boulder and every muscle in my body freezes, causing Riva to laugh harder. "Do you think he finally figured it out?"

"Girls...as in plural? As in more than one?"

Riva's smile reaches each side of her face as she nods. "We are having twins!"

I nearly pass out but somehow remain strong. I clasp my wife's face and bring her in for a crushing kiss. "I love you so much."

"Not as much as I love you, husband." She wiggles her nose against my chin and I know in that very moment that every adversity I faced in the swamp was worth it for her.

"I must go tell the other clan elders." Izel saunters out of our tree cabin almost in a happier daze than me. "This changes everything!"

# SNEAK PEEK

# CHAPTER 1: EVRIN

I rub my hand over my face in a feeble attempt to banish my exhaustion. I've been so tired ever since I spoke to Kal. He is our clan's animal trapper and was a fellow outcast who ended up catching a human female in one of his traps. The latest news is that she just gave birth to twin girls. I can't help the deep-seated jealousy brewing under my thick skin. Around a hundred years ago, the orc female population started to decline. The elders desperately searched for answers but found none. Since then, it was agreed that orc males would be an outcast from the clan when they came of age and could only return if they found a female to breed and wed. Normally, this would be another orc female, but since Kal's human wife gave birth to girls, our mating pool has widened. I want nothing more than to have a wife and kits, but I fear Kal's situation was merely a stroke of luck. How will I ever find a human mate if they are forbidden to enter the swamp we call home?

I try my best to expel the thoughts that have eaten away at me for the past few months. I must focus on the task at hand: meeting at the rendezvous point on the edge of the swamplands with one of my regular tradesmen. Orcs and humans don't typically trade with each other, but very little iron can be found in the swamps. As a blacksmith, that poses quite an issue. Normally, our swamp clan trades with an orc clan in the mountains. But since news of a wedded and bred human has reached them, they have cut off all communications. They are foolish orcs who believe the species should remain "pure". Gah! They have lost their minds. What a blessing it is to have a mate. Why anyone would reject such a bond for the simple sake of purity is beyond me.

But their lack of cooperation has forced me to work with the humans. Something I had hopes in which could lead me to find a female mate. However, I was sorely disappointed to discover every human tradesman is a male who doesn't have the guts to meet an orc face to face. Instead, we operate solely on a drop-and-collect basis. The only reason I know they are all males is because, for the first month, I watched them from afar. They are blissfully unaware of a predator that lurks in the distance. I must say that humans have terrible survival instincts.

Just as I reach my collection point, I hear rustling in nearby bushes. I reach for one of the swords strapped to my back and ready myself. We might just be outside the swamplands, but that doesn't stop some creatures. I round a tree, and my body stills. It is no creature. It is a human female. I quickly return my blade to my back and gape at her in stunned silence.

Her back faces me as she is crouched down, carefully picking berries and filling her woven basket. She has bright fire-colored hair, pale skin, and an ample bosom. My cock immediately stiffens at the sight of her. What is she doing this close to the swamplands? I am overjoyed by her presence but my immediate reaction is to protect her from the unknown dangers of the swamp. My question is quickly answered as I observe the small blue fruit in between her delicate fingers. They are swamp berries. They are delectable sweet fruits, but humans are generally unfamiliar with them. Understandably, they only grow in the swamp or near the swamplands.

I've never seen a human female before, and I swear I forget how to breathe momentarily. Everything about her is perfect: her thick thighs, her wide hips, and rosy red cheeks.

I've always been an orc of action, at least until now. Of course, I want to rut her into the ground, but I also want to observe her. Get to know her. What does her voice sound like when she is moaning my name? What will she make with those berries? Does she taste as sweet as she looks? I have a million questions, but I am not brave enough to ask one. So, instead, I watch her. She completes her work and is content with the now full basket of berries. None-the-wiser, this human female has no idea that an orc stalks her from a distance. My anxiety peaks at her lack of spatial awareness. Many dangers lurk in this world, waiting to strike against someone as delectable as her. I desire nothing more than to drag her back to my cabin, where I can keep her safe.

I follow her down a dirt path, close enough to keep her in my line of vision but not close enough to alert her to my presence. I've never ventured this far into the human lands before, but I'm entranced by this seductress. The hem of her dress drags along the road, dirtying it, but she doesn't seem to mind. By the looks of her blue tattered gown, she is used to working in this attire. Odd, why don't human females wear something more practical?

It doesn't take long until he arrives at a decaying cabin. Surely, this can't be where she lives. There appears to be no other human homes in sight. Where is her clan? Is she an outcast like me?

She stops in front of the door, and it creaks open. It is practically hanging off of its hinges. I get a glance at her face before she enters her home, and although it's stunning, there is a hint of sadness to it.

I'm completely enthralled by this woman, and the second I lose sight of her, I am desperate for more. I survey our surroundings and deem a nearby hill to be my best vantage point. I use bushes and trees to hide my presence and dance along the property line until I reach my spot.

"I guess I'm not completely useless," I whisper to myself and crouch into the position that looks directly into two windows. I gaze into what appears to be a poorly lit bedroom and a common room. Up until this point, it is like I have lost every skill I've learned over the last twenty-six years.

I see something move in the common room window and my body stills. I register the presence of a male. I already feel incredibly possessive over this female, and having another male nearby will turn ugly fast. I let out a growl. The second I laid eyes on her near the swamp I knew that will be my bride and the mother of my kits.

Before I grab one of the swords strapped to my back, the human male stumbles into a better view. I watch as he brings a metal container to his lips and sways around. The man is drunk and....way too old to be the human female's mate. This must be her father, then. I breathe a sigh of relief, although I'm still not happy he is in her presence. My sweet human doesn't seem to enjoy his company either; she looks upon him with apathy, not love.

What has happened to this poor creature to make her so sullen with her own loved ones? I would give nothing more than to have my parents back.

She places the basket of swamp berries on a table and saunters into the dark bedroom. I grunt in frustration, I can't see a thing, and my cock is begging to get a glimpse of her beautiful round figure.

Time passes, and I grow agitated with every moment. I double-check that her father stays in the common room; I would have no qualm killing him if he dared stumble into her room. Small candle light starts flickering as my human ignites them one by one. It takes my orc eyes time to adjust to the sudden change in brightness. I see pieces of her bright hair flicker into view and flashes of pale, freckled skin. Gah! This gods forsaken window is too small!

But just as my frustration peaks, my vision adjusts, and I see a floor-length mirror positioned perfectly for my viewing pleasure. She finally meanders in front of the mirror, and I have the best fucking angle of her fat ass and large breasts. She is wearing a white corset, some frilly white shorts, and stockings that taunt me. By the gods, I nearly come just at the sight of her. But something in the back of my mind starts to eat away at me. Why does her appearance unnerve me? My human looks at herself in the mirror, appreciating her hand-sculpted body from the gods, and it suddenly dawns on me.

Humans wear all white to their weddings.

I feel my face pale, and rages boil my veins. No, she will not be someother's bride. She is *mine*!

I take no time to think through my actions before I sprint down the short hill. I will not take any chances that this human weds another. For a split second, I debate, entering through the window. But I quickly realize I won't fit. The only opportunity to enter the cabin will be through the front door.

Without hesitation, I round the corner of the house and kick down the rotting door. I do not attempt subtly; this weak male and my sweet human are the only humans around.

"What the fuck-"the man screams and falls onto his

ass. Maybe seeing an orc in his unkempt home will sober him up.

"Uncle Edmund?" my redheaded human opens the door to the bedroom but screams as she registers my presence. Ah, he is her uncle, not her father.

"Ivy!" The human named Edmund shrieks.

"Ivy..." I play with her name on my tongue. Gorgeous, just like her.

I charge past Ivy's uncle as he struggles to his feet and barge through the bedroom door that she attempts to slam close. Ivy has both weight and height, but her strength is no match to mine.

"What do you want, you beast!" she yells.

I wince at her words. I want this sweet human to welcome me into her arms and body. At the moment, she is doing neither.

"You," I growl; I can't help my aggression. The idea of another male marrying my bride has me frayed at the edges.

"Me?" She whispers confused.

A sudden jolt of laughter sounds from the common room. Uncle Edmund laughs hysterically, "You want... Ivy? You can have her!"

Although he offers me what I desire the most, I can't help but to grind my teeth together. I look back towards Ivy, and her expression tells me enough. She stares at me like wild prey who knows they are about to be eaten. Her wide eye expression and rapid breaths show both her fear and her sadness.

"You would give up your own niece to a beast?" I ask with my voice laced with disgust. I know I will give Ivy the best life. She will be loved, protected, and cared for by me. But this cowered of a man doesn't know that.

"That whore? I've been trying to get rid of her for the past four years!"

"What did you call her?" I pull a sword from the back of my sheath and charge the drunk bastard. Ivy yells something, but I can't hear her. My ears ring, and my eyes blur with rage. Edmund, now on his feet, has found a blade of his own and does his best to match my strikes. It is clear he has had decent training yet he stands no chance against me. I block his every advance until I finally land a punch to his stomach. Edmund slouches over, and I take my opportunity to disarm him by slicing my blade through his right wrist. He won't ever pick up with that blade again.

"Fuck!!" He screams in pain, "my hand!"

"Don't worry, your head will soon be joining it," I grit out and raise my blade again to deliver the fatal blow.

"Don't kill him! Please!" Ivy begs as she runs towards me. My anger dims almost immediately, and I shift my focus to her.

"Please don't kill him! I will go with you," she begs "I promise, but just don't kill him. I've killed enough people in my family."

I don't understand what she is referring to, yet I can't deny my beautiful bride anything.

"But he disrespected you. It is an offense that can only be remedied with a battle to the death. I am protecting your honor." I try explaining myself. She will soon come to learn orc traditions.

"Honor? I don't have much of that these days," she whispers.

"My fucking hand!" Edmund cries, cradling his blooded stub.

I look down at the pathetic creature but ultimately succumb to my wife-to-be's wishes. Why she desires to keep her uncle alive after how he treats her is beyond me. I lower my bland and hear her sigh of relief. But not me. No, I have no form of relief. I'm currently a giant mass of tension. My anger and lust have reached a boiling point. It is time to return to the swamp. I slide my sword back into the sheath strapped to my back.

"Thank you-," she starts speaking, but I cut her off by wrapping my arm around her ass and throwing her over my shoulder, "HEY! Put me down!" Ivy shrieks.

Within a few strides we are exiting the small crumbling cabin with only her uncle's soft sobs lingering in the distance. Ivy beats on my back, calling me many names, but I pay her no mind. I finally have a bride. It might take her time to accept me. But soon enough I will have a wife full of my seed and a pussy that is all mine. I will no longer be an outcast.

## ORDER HERE

# JOIN MY PATREON

Interested in seeing NSFW art? Scan QR code below

*Join my Patreon*

# ALSO BY K.L. WYATT

Brides of the Frostwolf Clan Series

Stolen by the Orc Commander: An Enemies to Lovers
Monster Romance

*Also by K.L. Wyatt*

**Start reading <u>here</u>**

**A human girl set on revenge...**

Orcs and humans have been at war with each other for as long as Snow can remember. Orphaned as a child, she has spent her years as a tracker, known only as the 'Hooded Bandit' by the king's men. Stealing anything she can in order to survive the harsh human lands of Everdean. The only thing keeping her going is the determination to make those responsible for her family's death suffer.

When a routine carriage robbery goes south, Snow finds herself face to face with the notorious orc commander himself. Taken as his captive and returned to Orc Mountain, Snow has a new goal: escape from the mountain no matter the cost.

**An orc commander determined to end the war...**

Azogg the Destroyer is a skilled fighter. As leader of the orc army, he despises humans more than most. The war has destroyed their homelands, leaving them all to suffer in the mountains. As commander, he knows that he must find a way to end this conflict once and for all.

With no other choice, Azogg finds himself tracking a royal advisor...only to have his plans upended by a sickly human female. One he quickly discovers is not what she seems. Azogg is resistant to trusting a human, but her extensive knowledge of the royal trade routes makes her the ultimate find.

Could this human be the key to ending the war?

Tempers and passion flare as both Snow and Azogg realize the only way forward is for them to work together. Will this unlikely pair be able to put aside decades of hate and distrust? Or will factors beyond their control drive them apart before they get the chance?

**Welcome to Orc Mountain.**

**My Orc Valentine: A Brides of the Frostwolf Clan Novella**
**Book 1.5**

## Start Reading <u>here</u>

The orcs and humans have recently formed a tentative allyship, ending the decades long feud they have been locked in. Now, the two species are trying to navigate coexisting within their new world.

On the night of Lupercalia, a festival celebrating love, Lyra is shocked to see a group of orc soldiers arrive at the human brothel she works at. However, she can't afford to worry about the one who keeps casting curious looks her way. Lyra is freshly eighteen and in the spirit of the holiday her mistress has decided she would make the ultimate prize by auctioning off her virginity to the highest bidder. She is shocked when the male she caught staring at her earlier seems the most intent on winning her. The young orc soldier named Zhor soon out bids the others; his eyes promising a night of passion that Lyra won't ever forget.

As apprehension gives way to unbridled passion, Lyra grapples with the fact that the feelings growing between her and Zhor can only last the night. Even if she finds herself wishing Lupercalia never ends.

**Chained to Krampus: A Holiday Novella**

**Start Reading <u>here</u>**

With the Christmas season fast approaching, a decades-long tradition looms closer. A tradition that is as macabre as it is longstanding. For every seventy years, the townspeople must choose who amongst them is to be sacrificed to Krampus.

At twenty-seven years old, Holly is still a virgin and

determined to keep it that way. However, her life takes an unexpected turn when she rejects the town's mayor and is chosen as Krampus's sacrifice. Expecting to die at the hands of this cruel beast, Holly is shocked to learn that her new captor has different intentions in mind. Ones that will bind them together forever and leave her round with his child. Desperate for her freedom, she finds herself chained to the horrific creature as he seeks to claim more than just her body.

Despite his monstrous nature, Holly soon learns there is more to this Krampus than meets the eye.

Kristof, the only living Krampus, has lived alone for many years. Bound by his duty to continue his kind's lineage, he eagerly awaits the arrival of his human offering. When he meets his virgin sacrifice, she is nothing short of perfection. The only issue is that her feelings are not reciprocated. In fact, she recoils at his mere presence. When Holly tries to flee, he has no choice but to shackle her to him. Will Kristof be able to show his new mate that they are more similar than she thinks? Or will the chains that bind them only serve to drive them further apart?

# ABOUT THE AUTHOR

Kayla, is a smut obsessed 20-something year old, that didn't discover her love for books until later in life. Her new hobby soon became an obsession she wished to share with others and thus her Booktok account was created. Little did she know that this would change the trajectory of her life forever.

Now, two and half years later she has a new ambition, becoming a romance author. She loves all things monsters, but especially Orcs. Combining her beasts with fantasy, she hopes all of her readers have monster-loving time with her new series, Brides of the Frostwolf Clan.

Originally from the Midwest, Kayla works from home in her small Connecticut apartment with her boyfriend and two cats. When she isn't engrossed in her latest read, she is conducting Tarot readings for her friends, watching Love Island, and playing the Sims.

Keep up to date by signing up to my <u>newsletter!</u>